SIMPLE DEVICES

THE WEDGE

Patricia Armentrout

The Rourke Press, Inc.
Vero Beach, Florida 32964

Patricia Armentrout specializes in nonfiction writing and has had several book series published for primary schools. She resides in Cincinnati with her husband and two children.

PHOTOS CREDITS:
© Armentrout: pages 4, 9, 10, 15, 21; © East Coast Studios: pages 6, 7, 16; © James P. Rowan: page 12; © Mimi Cotter/Intl Stock: Cover; © Phyllis Picardi/Intl Stock: pages 13, 18; © James Broderick/Intl Stock: page 19; © Scott Barrow/Intl Stock: page 22;

EDITORIAL SERVICES:
Penworthy Learning Systems

Library of Congress Cataloging-in-Publication Data

Armentrout, Patricia, 1960-
  The wedge / Patricia Armentrout.
    p. cm. — (Simple Devices)
  Includes index
  Summary: Text and pictures introduce the wedge, a simple device placed between objects to split, tighten, or secure a hold.
  ISBN 1-57103-181-2
  1. Wedges—Juvenile literature. [1. Wedges.]
I. Title II. Series: Armentrout, Patricia, 1960- Simple Devices.
TJ1201.W44A76 1997
621.8'11—dc21
                                  97–15158
                                    CIP
                                    AC

Printed in the USA

TABLE OF CONTENTS

DEVICES

Most people like **devices** (deh VYS ez). Devices make work and play easier.

Woodworkers use devices. Homemakers use devices. In fact, you can find devices in just about every home and business.

Devices that have many parts are **complex** (KAHM pleks) devices. A car and a washing device are complex devices.

The blade on a garden trowel is a kind of wedge.

SIMPLE DEVICES

Six devices invented long ago are still used today. They are the wheel, the screw, the lever, the pulley, the inclined plane, and the **wedge** (WEJ).

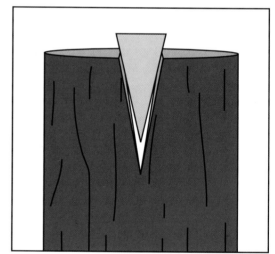

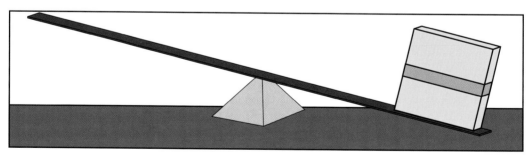

The pulley, wedge, and lever are simple devices.

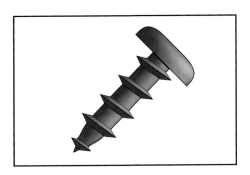

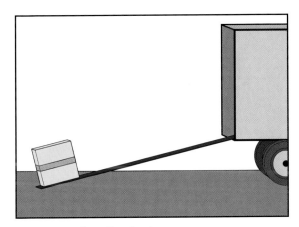

The wheel, screw, and inclined plane are simple devices.

These simple devices have few parts and work without fuel or electricity. They do simple jobs, but they make life a whole lot better for people.

This book explores the wedge, a simple device that many people use every day.

THE WEDGE

A wedge can be used to split, tighten, or secure a hold. All wedges use force to come between things, but they are not always called a wedge.

A wedge that is called a wedge is a simple iron tool. An iron wedge is shaped like a triangle. The thinnest, or narrowest, end of the wedge is used to split logs and rocks.

Force is applied at the widest end of the wedge, usually with a large hammer, and the narrow end is forced into wood or rock.

An iron wedge is a simple device used to split rock or wood.

A WEDGE THAT SPLITS

The iron wedge is a wedge used to split. Can you think of another metal object used to split wood? If you came up with the ax, you are right.

An ax is a tool that is a wedge. The ax is driven, by muscle power, to split logs. Can you imagine how hard it would be to split logs without an ax or an iron wedge?

You use a wedge every time you bite into an apple. That's right, your teeth can work like a wedge. They split the apple while your jaw muscles exert the force.

An ax is a splitting tool.

WEDGES THAT CUT

Wedges that cut work the same way as a splitting iron wedge. They too use force to come between things to cut them apart.

The sharp teeth on a saw blade are cutting wedges.

A woodcarver uses a chisel to carve a wooden sign.

A kitchen knife is a cutting wedge. People use it every day to slice bread or carve a turkey. A handsaw is a tool that works as a wedge. The tiny metal teeth are little wedges that cut into wood and split it in two. **Chisels** (CHIZ elz) are also wedges used to cut, or chip, away pieces of wood.

These simple cutting tools are the basis of more complex power cutting tools.

A WEDGE THAT TIGHTENS

You may have heard the words "wedged in." It probably makes you think of someone stuck in a tight place. A wedge is not only used for splitting and cutting—it is also used to tighten.

A doorstop is a wedge used for tightening. A rubber or wooden triangle-shaped doorstop is a useful device that can be bought at most hardware stores. It easily holds a door open when wedged between the floor and the bottom of a door.

A door stop is wedged between the floor and the bottom of the door.

A WEDGE THAT HOLDS

Can you think of a wedge that holds two things together? Hint: It's found in many home tool boxes. Did you guess the nail?

A nail is made with a pointed end to break the surface of wood. The driving force of a hammer wedges the nail into the wood and attaches the wood to a wall or other wood.

A nail is a wedge that holds two or more objects together.

A MOVEABLE DEVICE

The wedge is a simple device that works by being moved. The ax and iron wedge work when they are forced into the wood. The doorstop can be moved easily when no longer needed. The nail moves when hammered into wood. Saw blades cut when moved back and forth.

An engine powers this cutting device.

A sewing machine needle is a fast moving wedge.

A simple moving wedge can also be part of a more complex device. Think about the sewing machine. A needle moves and splits fabric apart as it carries the thread through.

HEAVY-DUTY WEDGES

So far you have read about small, simple objects that are wedges. Some heavy-duty devices work as wedges too.

Every day construction workers use wedges to clear land and dig holes. They use the sharp blades of a bulldozer and power shovel to cut away chunks of earth.

The splitting, holding, and tightening action of the wedge is used everywhere. Can you find more examples of the simple device called the wedge?

The big shovel on a front-end loader can scoop up hundreds of pounds of dirt.

GLOSSARY

chisels (CHIZ elz) — sharp-edged metal tools used to cut and shape materials

complex (KAHM pleks) — made up of many parts or elements

device (deh VYS) — an object, such as a lever, pulley, or inclined plane, used to do one or more simple tasks

wedge (WEJ) — a simple device placed between objects to split, tighten, or secure a hold

The blade on a snow shovel works like a wedge.

INDEX